First printed 1997
Reprinted 1998, 1999, 2000

ISBN 1 85534 765 2

Printed and bound in Slovenia

IRISH LEGENDS

The Salmon of Knowledge

Retold by Reg Keating
Illustrated by Heather McKay

Tarantula Books

Finegas was a poet. He was one of the wisest men in all Ireland.

He lived in a small, stone house by the banks of the River Boyne. Finegas had built the house himself many years before.

He lived there alone, reading books and writing poetry.

For many years, Finegas stayed by the banks of the river. He watched carefully for a fish called the Salmon of Knowledge.

Finegas knew that the Salmon was a magic fish.

The first person to taste the Salmon would become the wisest person in all Ireland.

The Salmon of Knowledge was enormous. It had skin that was the colour of gold. Its eyes had magical powers.

Many people had tried to catch it, but had failed.

Finegas wanted to be the first to catch the Salmon.

If he did, he would certainly be the wisest man in Ireland.

In the old days, there were no schools in Ireland. Instead of going to school, young warriors were taught by wise men like Finegas.

Young men would go to live with a poet. There, they would learn poetry, storytelling and many other skills.

After this training, the young men could become true warriors.

Finn was the son of a great warrior named Cumhall.

Finn was a tall, handsome young man with fair hair and blue eyes.

He was training to be a warrior like his father.

Because of this, Finn was sent to live with Finegas the poet.

One day, Finegas was sitting by the river, teaching poetry to Finn.

Suddenly, Finegas saw a huge, powerful fish swimming in the river. It was the Salmon of Knowledge!

Finegas was very excited. He had never seen such a beautiful creature before.

He ran as fast as he could to get a strong net to catch the fish.

Finn was sitting with his back to the river. He was learning his poetry and did not see the Salmon.

The Salmon of Knowledge had special magic powers. If a person looked at its eyes, that person would fall into a deep sleep.

Finegas knew this. He was very careful not to look at the Salmon's eyes.

For hours and hours, Finegas tried to catch the Salmon, but it was too strong and fast for him.

All of a sudden, the Salmon jumped high into the air towards Finegas.

The old poet was taken by surprise. He stared at the fish. At once, he fell fast asleep.

Finn saw what had happened. He rushed to wake Finegas before the Salmon escaped.

When Finegas awoke, he asked Finn to fetch him a piece of cloth.

Finn did as he was told.

Then, Finegas covered his eyes with the cloth. He went over to the river and threw in his net again.

For hours and hours more he tried to catch the fish, but could not.

As night was falling, he decided to have one last try.

This time he was lucky. He caught the Salmon in his net.

But the fight was not over! The huge fish struggled and struggled to get out of the net. It jumped and pulled, tossed and turned, but could not escape.

After many hours of battling, Finegas had finally caught the Salmon of Knowledge.

Finegas was very, very tired. Because of this, he told Finn to cook the Salmon.

Finegas warned Finn that he was not to eat even a mouthful of the fish.

Finn promised that he would not eat any of the salmon.

He built a big fire with sticks and leaves. He lit the fire and waited until it was burning merrily.

Then Finn placed the fish over the open fire.

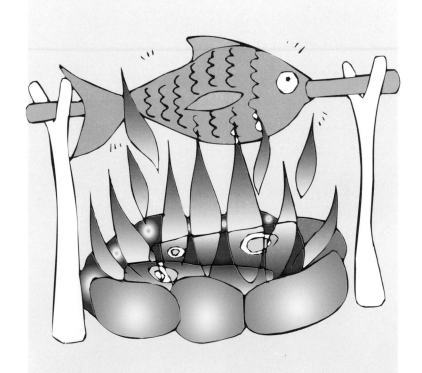

Soon the Salmon was almost ready to be eaten.

Suddenly, a drop of burning oil from the fish splashed onto Finn's thumb.

Without thinking, Finn put his thumb into his mouth to ease the pain.

When the Salmon was cooked, Finn took it to Finegas.

The wise old poet noticed that Finn looked a little different.

His eyes were brighter than before and his cheeks were redder.

"Have you eaten any of the Salmon?" Finegas asked Finn.

Finn told him the truth.

"No, I have not," Finn said. "I gave you my word that I would not".

Finegas was still not happy.

"Have you even tasted the salmon?" he asked.

Then Finn remembered that he had burnt his thumb and put it in his mouth. He told this to Finegas.

The old poet knew at once that the wisdom of the Salmon had been given to Finn.

At first Finegas was very sad. He knew now that he would never be the wisest man in Ireland.

But he was happy that it was Finn, his favourite student, who had been given the gift.

Finegas knew that Finn would become the greatest leader that the Fianna had ever known.